Judy Moody Goes to College

Megan McDonald is the award-winning author of the Judy Moody series. She says that most of Judy's stories "grew out of anecdotes about growing up with my four sisters". She confesses, "I am Judy Moody. Same-same! In my family of sisters, we're famous for exaggeration. Judy Moody is me … exaggerated." Megan McDonald lives with her husband in northern California.

You can find out more about Megan McDonald and her books at **www.meganmcdonald.net**

Peter H. Reynolds says he felt an immediate connection to Judy Moody because "having a daughter, I have witnessed first-hand the adventures of a very independent-minded girl". Peter H. Reynolds lives in Massachusetts, just down the road from his twin brother.

You can find out more about Peter H. Reynolds and his art at **www.fablevision.com**

Books by Megan McDonald
and Peter H. Reynolds

Judy Moody
Judy Moody Gets Famous!
Judy Moody Saves the World!
Judy Moody Predicts the Future
Judy Moody: The Doctor Is In!
Judy Moody Declares Independence!
Judy Moody: Around the World in 8 1/2 Days
Judy Moody Goes to College
Judy Moody, Girl Detective
Judy Moody and the NOT Bummer Summer
Judy Moody and the Bad Luck Charm
Stink: The Incredible Shrinking Kid
Stink and the Incredible Super-Galactic Jawbreaker
Stink and the World's Worst Super-Stinky Sneakers
Stink and the Great Guinea Pig Express
Stink: Solar System Superhero
Stink and the Ultimate Thumb-Wrestling Smackdown
Stink and the Midnight Zombie Walk
Stink and the Freaky Frog Freakout
Stink-O-Pedia: Super Stink-y Stuff from A to Zzzzz
Stink-O-Pedia 2: More Stink-y Stuff from A to Z
Judy Moody & Stink: The Holly Joliday
Judy Moody & Stink: The Mad, Mad, Mad,
Mad Treasure Hunt

Books by Megan McDonald

Ant and Honey Bee: What a Pair!
The Sisters Club
The Sisters Club: Rule of Three
The Sisters Club: Cloudy with a Chance of Boys

Books by Peter H. Reynolds

The Dot • Ish • So Few of Me

Judy Moody
Goes To College

Megan McDonald

illustrated by
Peter H. Reynolds

WALKER
BOOKS

First published 2009 by Walker Books Ltd
87 Vauxhall Walk, London SE11 5HJ

This edition published 2011

30

Text © 2008 Megan McDonald
Illustrations © 2008 Peter H. Reynolds
Judy Moody font © 2003 Peter H. Reynolds

This book has been typeset in Stone Informal

Printed and bound in Great Britain by Clays Ltd, St Ives plc

British Library Cataloguing in Publication Data:
a catalogue record for this book
is available from the British Library

ISBN 978-1-4063-3589-7

www.walker.co.uk

For Sophia and Emily
M. M.

Dedicated to Beatrice Rose Scollan,
Desmond Patrick Scollan and Beth "Ginger
Betty" Veneto, who deserve honorary degrees
for their community service!
P. H. R.

Table of Contents

Judy Moody

Tutor tot.
Rare to the power of ten.

Who's

Dad

aka Richard.
Old skool.

Mum

aka Kate.
One-half of the 'rents.

Mouse
Yoga (not yoghurt) Cat.

Who

Stink
The original geck = annoying person.

Frank

The peeps.

Chloe

Sick-awesome college student. Judy's *uber*-rare tutor.

Rocky

Math-i-tude

When Judy Moody got to school on Monday,
she had a new teacher. Her new teacher
was called a sub (not the sandwich). Her
new teacher was called Mrs Grossman.
Exactly three things were wrong with
that. (1) Mrs *Gross*man was NOT gross. (2)
Mrs Gross*man* was NOT a man. (3) Mrs
Grossman was NOT Mr Todd.

Judy was the first to raise her hand.
"Where's Mr Todd?"

"I'm sure Mr Todd told everyone on Friday that he was going to a special teachers' conference."

"I wasn't here on Friday," said Judy.

"He's going to learn to be a better teacher," said Jessica Finch.

"But Mr Todd's already a great teacher," said Judy.

"Maybe he's getting a special teacher's award," said Rocky.

"Where did he go?" Judy asked. "And when will he be back?"

The others joined in. "Are you going to read us *Catwings*? Mr Todd always reads us *Catwings*. And *Catwings Return*."

"Are you going to take us on school trips? Mr Todd always takes us on school trips."

"Are we still Class 3T? Or are we Class 3G now?"

"Mr Todd is in Bologna in Italy," said Mrs Grossman.

Sheesh. Life was no fair. Judy liked baloney (in her sandwiches). Judy liked Italy. She even knew a special dance from Italy – the tarantella. Mr Todd was probably in the Land of Baloney right now, dancing like a tarantula, while they were stuck in the Land of Multiplication, learning boring old times tables.

She, Judy Moody, did not like third grade, Class 3T-that-was-now-3G, without Mr Todd.

Judy Moody's new teacher came from

New England. She did not talk like Mr
Todd. She talked funny, with a lot of extra
rs. Judy Moody's new teacher did not
wear cool glasses like Mr Todd. She wore
glasses hanging from a chain round her
neck. She did not even smell like Mr Todd.
She smelled like she took a bath in P.U.
perfume.

Judy Moody's new teacher put up a
tent at the back of the room with a sign
that said ATTITUDE TENT. Judy wondered
what attitude they had to be in to get to go
camping.

And ... Judy Moody's new teacher was
screwy for sweets. She gave out sweets for
good behaviour to everybody (minus Judy,

because she was in a mood). She even gave out sweets for the right answers in maths. Pretty soon, the whole class was going to have maths cavities. Except for Judy.

Today, Mrs Grossman was talking about measurements. Litres and millilitres and barrels and hogsheads. She tried to make it sound like maths was a barrel of fun. But Judy, for one, did not give a pig's ear about hogsheads.

Mrs Grossman wore ten gallons of perfume.
Mrs Grossman gave out twenty hogsheads of sweets.

Instead of listening, Judy played with her watch. Her brand-new, fancy-dancy, duck-egg-blue, glow-in-the-dark Ask-a-Question

Watch 5000, complete with predict-the-future answers and screen saver.

Blah, blah, blah, said Mrs Grossman. Rounding numbers up, rounding numbers down. Judy *estimated* that *rounding* did not make maths one bit easier.

Judy pressed some buttons. A night light blinked. A dual-time button gave the time in TWO countries so a person did not have to wear two different watches.

Scribble, scribble. Mrs Grossman scratched on the board for a math-ternity.

Judy pressed the big green question-mark button.

Rare! It was just like the Magic 8 Ball. Ask the watch a question, press the glow-in-the-dark green button and it gave you mystery answers.

Is Mrs Grossman cuckoo for maths?

YOU BET.

Is Mrs Grossman ever going to give me a sweet?

CAN'T TELL.

Am I going to college someday?

LOOKS GOOD.

Is Mr Todd ever coming back?

HAZY.

"Judy? Did you hear the question?"

Judy did not hear the question. So Judy did not know the answer.

Was it 77? 88? 99? Litres? Bathtubs? Barrels? Pigs' heads?

Judy blurted the only answer that sprang to mind.

"Hazy!" she called out.

Mum- and Dad-i-tude

She, Judy Moody, had to take a note home.
A note from the teacher. A note that said
she needed extra-special help. A note that
said she was hazy-not-crazy about maths.

The top half of the note was just *blah-
blah,* so Judy tore it in half and gave the
good half to her parents. Not the bad half.
Mum and Dad looked at the note.

"Judy's in trouble? Sweet!" said Stink.

"Only *half* trouble," said Judy.

"Judy, where's the rest of this note?" asked Dad.

"I rounded it down," said Judy. "To one-half. Like the fraction. Get it? I'm really good at maths. Fractions and rounding and everything."

"Quick! What's twelve times eight?" asked Stink.

"None of your beeswax," said Judy.

"Try ninety-six," said Stink.

"Judy, the note?" Mum said. "Dad and I need to see it. The *whole* thing."

Judy reached into her pocket and pulled out the crumpled-up bottom half of the note. She handed it over.

Mum and Dad read it. They read it times two. It took them about one thousand years to read the fraction of a note.

They talked to Judy. They talked to each other. They talked to people on the phone for a hundred years. They came up with a plan.

Not a Listen-to-Your-New-Teacher plan.

Not a Hand-Over-Your-Brand-New-Watch plan.

Not a We'll-Help-You-with-Your-Homework plan.

An Extra-Extra-Special-Help plan. *EESH!* A Judy-Moody-Goes-to-a-Tutor plan.

"Tutor?" said Judy. "Can't you and Dad help me?"

"We will," said Mum.

"We will," said Dad.

"What's six times seven?" said Stink.

"A tutor will be extra help," said Mum.

"A tutor will be special help," said Dad. "Just like your teacher suggested."

"For your information," said Judy, "Mrs Grossman is NOT my teacher."

"What's five times eleven?" asked Stink.

"I'll listen, I promise," said Judy. "I won't wear my new watch to school any more. I'll count to gross and great gross."

"*You're* gross," said Stink.

Judy had to prove she was good at maths. She started rattling off times tables.

"Four times two is eight. Eight times two

is sixteen. Sixteen times two is something I haven't learned yet. But I will. I swear."

"Having a tutor could be fun," said Dad. "You'll see."

"*Tutors* have *flash cards,*" said Stink. "*Baby* flash cards. What's two times five?"

"The number of toenails I'm going to paint while you're asleep," said Judy. Stink curled his toes under.

Judy looked from Mum to Dad, from Dad to Mum. "Do I have to?"

"It's already settled," said Mum. "You start tomorrow."

"Hogsheads!" said Judy.

Dad picked Judy up from school the next day. Judy closed her eyes and slumped in the back seat of the car on the way to the tutor's. All she could see behind her closed eyes were flash cards. *Baby* flash cards. She, Judy Moody, was in a mood. Not a maths mood. And definitely NOT a flash card mood.

Fact of Life: She, Judy Moody, was a Tutor Tot.

"Am I going to have to count beads and glue macaroni? Stink says I am going to have to count beads and glue macaroni."

"I don't know," said Dad.

"Am I going to have to play with jelly beans in jars? Stink says I'm going to have to play with jelly beans in jars," said Judy.

"I don't know," said Dad.

"Am I going to have to make a cat out of a triangle? Stink says I'm going to have to make a cat out of a triangle."

"Let's wait and see," said Dad. "Maybe you'll get to play maths games – like tic-tac-toe."

Tic-tac-toe-nails! Judy made a mad face and slumped down in the seat some more. Dad didn't get it. He didn't have to spend his afternoon doing macaroni maths and making geometry cats.

"We're here!" Dad called cheerfully.

"Where's here?" Judy asked in a moody tone.

"Colonial College," said Dad.

"College?" asked Judy.

"That's where you're getting help with your maths," said Dad. "Your tutor is a college student."

Judy bolted upright and threw her arms in the air. "I'm going to college!"

Mad-i-tude

Judy followed Dad down the tree-lined streets of the Colonial College campus, stepping on every crack she could find *on purpose.* They went past a duck pond with a fountain, a serious library with a clock tower and a way-cool giant sculpture of bacon and eggs. Finally, they came to a four-storey brick building with pointy towers that looked like a castle covered in ivy.

"This is it," said Dad. "Grace Brewster Murray Hopper Hall."

They wound their way upstairs and down long corridors to a door that said MATHS DEPARTMENT.

"Here we are!" said Dad.

A girl with green eyes and a messy ponytail greeted them. "You must be the Moodys."

"I'm Richard Moody, and this is my daughter, Judy," said Dad.

"Hi, I'm Chloe. Chloe Canfield. My friends call me C-squared, since my name has two Cs and I go to CC. You know, *C* to the power of two, 'cos I'm into maths?"

"That's funny," said Dad, shaking her hand.

"I don't get it," said Judy.

"It's algebra," Chloe said.

"Algebra? Didn't any-body tell you? I'm only in third grade."

Chloe laughed. "It just means when you multiply something by itself, you say it's squared, or to the power of two."

"Oh, yeah. If I'm in a mood, like a double bad mood, then it's called a bad mood squared, right?"

"That's right. Moody to the power of two," said Chloe. Dad bit his lip.

"Rounding off, squaring stuff and big powers – yikes!" said Judy.

"That's what I'm here for," said Chloe. "Maths is everywhere. Maths is a fact of life. You'll see. It'll be fun."

"I don't know." Judy saw flash cards on the table. Where there were flash cards, triangle cats and macaroni could not be far behind.

"You'll be fine," said Dad, smoothing the top of Judy's hair. But Judy wasn't so sure. "I'll be back in an hour to pick you up."

"That's sixty whole minutes!" Judy cried.

"Yep. Three thousand six hundred seconds." Chloe led Judy over to an area where a table was piled high with sponge blocks, coloured tiles and (oh, no!) jars of counting beads. For a split second, Judy had thought college was going to be cool. But this was *baby* college.

She, Judy Moody, was in a mood. Not a good mood. A bad mood squared. Moody to the power of ten million.

"This is the Investigation Station," said Chloe.

Investigation Station was probably just another name for *Homework* Station.

"What looks good?" Chloe asked, pointing to shelves against the walls stuffed with games.

"You mean we get to play a game and I get to pick and we don't have to count jelly beans in a jar?"

"I knew if I made you paper – you know, fill out work sheets – you'd freak. I thought you'd be all over playing a game. Then we'd be crucial."

"Kru-shul?"

"You know, good. Awesome."

"Oh, you mean *rare*. Let's play the Game of Life. It has a way-cool spinner."

"Rad," said Chloe. She tucked the box under her arm. "Let's go."

"Go where? Aren't we already there? At the Investigation Station?"

"I know a better place to study maths. It's called Coffee Catz."

Judy followed Chloe into the college coffee shop. Yum! It smelled like just-baked cookies and was packed with college kids reading, studying and madly typing on laptops.

Chloe ordered a tall, skinny, non-fat, wet, extra-foam, no-whip latte with a double shot of vanilla (aka fancy-schmancy coffee drink), and Judy ordered a hot chocolate in a *bowl*. Chloe gave Judy a ten-dollar bill, and Judy got to pay like a grown-up and count the change. There was enough change to buy a chocolate mobile phone at the counter.

At a window seat, Chloe spread out the board and Judy helped her snap in the mountains, bridges and buildings.

Chloe gave Judy a car to drive (round the board, that is). "I love this game, because it's like life. You get to go to college and make money and buy a house."

"Rare," said Judy. "I already know I want to be a doctor."

"For serious?" Chloe asked. "In the game or in life?"

"Both," said Judy.

"So, you're pre-med. That's what they call it before you go to medical school. Or in your case, pre-pre-med."

"Pre-med squared," said Judy.

"One of my peeps wants to be a doctor," said Chloe.

"Peeps?"

"One of my friends. You know, if you're going to go to college, you're gonna have to learn to *talk* college."

"For serious?" Judy asked.

"*Zing!* You got me there," said Chloe, laughing.

In the Game of Life, Judy got to be the banker. "My little brother, Stink, ALWAYS gets to be banker," she told Chloe. She,

Judy-Moody-not-Stink, was in charge of piles and piles of money and got to dish out the big bucks. AND Chloe let her be a doctor, even though it was against the rules to peek at the Career Cards.

Judy got to make a mountain of money and get married and buy a house and a high-definition TV and learn sign language and find buried treasure and go to the Grand Canyon and help the homeless, and not once did a tree fall on her; not even a mid-life crisis.

"I love Life!" said Judy.

"You beat the socks off me," said Chloe.

"Speaking of socks," said Judy, "can I ask you a question? Why are you wearing a dress and jeans and *no* socks?"

"It's my thing," said Chloe. "It's the artist in me."

"Is that why you wear flip-flops and have holes in your jeans and a flower tattoo and dyed-red hair and seven piercings?" Judy asked.

"Um, I guess so," said Chloe.

"Crucial!" said Judy.

On the way back to the Maths Department, Chloe and Judy cut through the car park. "Look at all the VW Beetles!" said Judy. "One green, two red, blue, yellow. My brother would go punch-buggy crazy!"

"So you like VW bugs?" Chloe asked. "Mine's the green one, right over there.

They call that colour Gecko Green. I call her June Bug, because I got her last June."

"For serious? Sweet! It even has a vase on the dashboard. Hey, did you know you're growing a toothbrush in your vase?" Judy cracked up.

"Tell you what," said Chloe. "Let's count all the Beetles in the car park and write down how many we can find of each colour. Then we'll go back to the department and I'll show you how to draw a graph."

Judy raced around the car park, counting lots of red, yellow and green bugs. Only two silver beetles, one blue and one grey. "The grey one looks like a robot!" said Judy.

Back in the Maths Department, Judy drew a graph and coloured in squares for each kind of Beetle. Salsa Red, Laser Blue, Sunflower Yellow… Judy forgot all about the time.

"Richard's here," said Chloe, nodding towards the door.

"Who's Richard?" Judy looked up and saw her dad standing in the doorway. "Is an hour up already?" she asked. "You were only gone for like a giga-flip-flop-second. Can't you stay away a little longer?"

"Having fun with maths, huh?"

"I'm learning to draw a graph, and when we've finished, Chloe says I can hang it on the wall. It'll be graph-iti!"

A New Attitude

Judy could not wait to go back to college – three times a week! Having a tutor was *crucial.* Rare squared!

In just two short weeks, Judy had found a brand-new lease of life.

She, Judy Moody, sashayed into the kitchen one morning before school. She was wearing a dress over jeans ripped at the knee, a teeny tiny hoodie, monkey flip-flops, a crazy scarf, skinny glasses, half a ton of bracelets and tattoo Band-Aids.

"She must be in a play," said Stink.

"That's ridonkulous," said Judy. "Unless you mean the play of *life*."

"How many tops are you wearing?" Stink asked.

"Is that my scarf?" Mum asked.

"I'm dressing for college," said Judy. "I'm going to my tutor after school today, Kate." Chloe called grown-ups by their first names, so Judy tried it.

"It's too cold for flip-flops," Mum said, frowning.

"And you'll need a coat," Dad added.

Parents. Parental Units. The 'Rents. Kate

and Richard were so *old skool*. "College kids don't wear coats!" said Judy.

"What do they wear?" asked Stink.

"They wear whatever's their thing," said Judy.

"So your thing is to dress like a clown?" Stink asked.

Eesh! What an NCP. Nincompoop.

"How's it going with Chloe, by the way?" Mum asked.

"Chloe is the bomb! She drives a green gecko Beetle called June Bug and has fake red hair, a toe ring and seven piercings."

"Nobody needs that many extra holes in their head," said Dad.

"What a Swiss Cheese Head!" said Stink. "I already have seven holes in my head.

Two eyes plus two ears plus two nostrils plus one mouth equals seven."

"Does this Chloe know any maths?" Mum asked.

"Does this Chloe have any flash cards?" asked Stink.

"For your information, we don't use flash cards," said Judy. "But we do play Multiplication Bingo and Tic-Tac-Cookie with Oreos. We even made a giant Sponge-Block Triangle Pants, and Chloe named him Nerd Ferguson." Judy snorted. "It was so *money*."

"I don't see what a sponge named Nerd Ferguson has to do with maths," said Stink. "Right, Mum? Right, Dad?"

Fact of Life: Stink = annoying!

"Stink, it's sponge *blocks*. They were invented by a kid. See, you add up all the lines and angles, and it makes a polygon. You can use triangles, rectangles and squares too." Mum raised her eyebrows at Dad. Dad raised his eyebrows at Mum.

"Aw," said Stink. "Can I go to college too?"

Judy ignored him. "Chloe says you can't be afraid of maths," she told Kate and Richard. "You just have to practise, like piano, or football. *And* you can't give up. *And* you have to remember to have fun."

"Well, I like your attitude," said Mum.

"You mean my *math*-i-tude," said Judy, cracking herself up. "Chloe says maths is everywhere. Maths is life."

"Then you'd better get going," said Mum. "Don't want to be late for life."

◈   ◈   ◈

On the way to school, Judy asked a question of her Ask-a-Question Watch 5000.

Will Mr Todd be back today? She pressed the green button.

`DON'T KNOW.`

She tried again. *Will Mr Todd be back today?*

`CAN'T TELL.`

She tried a third time. *Will Mr Todd be back today?*

`NO WAY!`

When she got to school, she raced down the corridor to her classroom. No Mr Todd. No fair.

Mrs Not-So-Great Grossman did not seem to appreciate Judy's new maths-is-everywhere take on life. To make things even worse, she told the class that Mr Todd had broken his foot in Italy. (Probably from dancing the tarantella.) Mr Todd would not be coming back for two more weeks.

As for the peeps, well, her friends were so UN-college. When they saw Judy's new outfit, they thought she was a scarecrow.

"What happened to your knees?" asked Rocky.

"Did you fall off your bike and rip your trousers?" Frank asked.

"It must have hurt a lot – look at all those Band-Aids," said Amy Namey.

"Tattoos," Judy muttered.

"It's just a phase," said Rocky. "Like when she wore her pyjamas to school."

"And her doctor's coat," said Frank.

"And her pilgrim outfit," said Jessica Finch.

"For your information," Judy pointed out, "kids in college wear pyjamas to class all the time. It's *rad*."

"It's red?" Rocky asked.

"It's rude?" Frank asked.

Sometimes third-graders were such *NCPs*.

"What stuff do you do with your tutor?" Amy asked.

"College stuff," said Judy. "We talk about algebra and—"

"Algebra?!" said Jessica Finch. "Even I don't know algebra."

"It's no biggie. When I hang out with my college friend, I get to drink coffee and drive a car and talk on a mobile phone."

"Whoa squared," said Amy Namey.

"Exactly," said Judy.

"You drink coffee?" asked Rocky.

"Actually, it's hot chocolate. But I do get to drink it in a coffee shop and order it and pay for it myself and count the change."

"Wow!" said Frank.

"No way did you drive a car," said Rocky.

"Yah-huh," said Judy. "No lie."

"You'd have to sit on like three phone books," said Frank.

"And get a licence," said Jessica Finch.

"I got to drive a car in the Game of Life," said Judy.

"Oh," said Rocky. Amy and Jessica rolled their eyes.

"Judy does know how to drive," said Frank. "She's driving ... us crazy!" Everybody cracked up.

Brat-i-tude

At morning break, Judy made a fake call on her chocolate mobile phone. During Science, Judy drew a cartoon of Mrs Grossman using polygons.

At lunchtime, Judy said, "Let's food!" and waited in the lunch queue with her peeps. When it was her turn, she stepped up to the counter and said to the dinner lady, "I'll have a small-tall upside-down backwards non-fat capp, extra whip. And make it wet."

"Aren't all drinks wet?" asked Frank.

"We don't have coffee," said the dinner lady.

"Hot chocolate?" Judy asked. But all they had was chocolate milk. *Bor-ing.* "At college, you can get hot chocolate with a heart design in the foam on top. And you can get sprinkles."

"Oh, really?" said the dinner lady.

"How many kinds of cereal do you have here?" Judy asked.

"None. We don't have any cereal. It's lunch."

"At college, you can have breakfast all

day. Even if it's midnight." Rocky, Frank and Jessica pushed past Judy.

"Do you have a salad bar?" Judy asked.

"The salad bar is only for teachers."

"At college, anybody can eat at the salad bar. Even kids. What kind of cafeteria is this? They should call it cafe*terrible.*"

"Hey, College!" yelled a fifth-grader at the back of the queue. "Move it along. Some of us want to eat lunch today."

Judy took her not-wet, no-whip, heartless chocolate milk and went to sit with her peeps.

"Shh, here she comes."

"What's she going to brag about now?"

"Yeah, she thinks she's so *college.*"

Soon she, Judy Moody, was eating alone at the lunch table. Fact of Life: Judy minus Rocky minus Frank minus Jessica Finch minus Amy Namey equals a big fat zero. Not a *peep*.

Judy stared at her lunch tray. Her peanut butter and jam sandwich looked so ... babyish.

At breaktime, nobody wanted to play Judy's game – finding polygons hidden in the playground. Judy found a triangle in a tree branch, an octagon where the fence was ripped and six rectangles on the ladder going up to the slide.

All by herself.

For the first time ever, Judy could not wait for her maths lesson. She, Judy Moody, *owned* the times tables. *Look out. Here comes the Multiplication Maniac. The Polygon Princess. The Graph Guru. The Fraction Freak. Just wait till they see me score sweets for all the right answers.*

At last it was time. Mrs Grossman started writing on the board. Judy sat up straight. She pricked up her best-ever listening ears, the ones she usually saved for Mr Todd. She squinted at the board.

Words? Why was Mrs Grossman writing so many words? What did words have to do with maths? *Hello?* Where were all the numbers?

And the fractions and the plus signs and the equal signs?

Judy raised her hand. "Excuse me," she said. "I thought this was a maths lesson. What's with all the sentences?"

"We're starting something new today," said Mrs Grossman. "Multistep word problems. You have to read the problem first, and then do the maths one step at a time. That's why we call them *word* problems."

Judy had a word problem, all right. A problem with words that were pretending to be maths.

Mrs Grossman pointed to the board. "Jill had twenty-four valentines. She gave half of her valentines to her friends at school—"

Judy raised her hand again. "Who's Jill?"

"Jill isn't a real person. She's just somebody in a word problem."

"So her name could be Chloe," said Judy. "And her school could be a college."

Mrs Grossman shut her eyes and took a deep breath. "Judy, please let me finish. Then Jill gave the other half of her valentines to friends who live in her block, except for—"

Judy raised her hand again. "Block? Like maybe a dorm?"

"It doesn't matter. It's just an example."

"Will we get to draw a graph for this

word problem? With hearts for valentines?" asked Judy. "Because in college we get to draw graphs."

"Judy, I'm going to have to ask you again to stop interrupting."

"I was just saying…" said Judy.

Mrs Grossman let out a big breath, but her face looked all pinched up. "Jill had enough valentines left over to give one each to her mum, her dad and her little sister."

"Jill sounds like an NCP," said Judy.

"Judy, that's it," said Mrs Grossman. She pointed to the tent at the back of the room.

"You mean I have to go in that tent?"

"That's why we call it the Attitude Tent," said Mrs Grossman.

"But I'm not really in a camping attitude," said Judy.

"Go and sit in the tent. Don't come out until you can show me an attitude adjustment. And not another word about college, Judy."

Eesh! Mrs Grossman was the reason she went to college in the first place. She wished Mrs Grossman would go back to where she came from. New England. Probably *Math*-a-chu-setts.

Judy hung her head and slunk to the back of the room. She crawled inside the tent. It was kind of like the Toad Pee Club clubhouse inside. Minus any peeing toads, of course. *Natch.*

She, Judy Moody, did not even play

with her Ask-a-Question Watch 5000. She thought about what she'd done, but she could not for the life of her understand why Mrs Grossman didn't like her attitude. Didn't she know a positive math-i-tude when she saw one?

Now Judy's math-i-tude had turned into a *mad*-i-tude.

Maths was no fair. Maths = life. Life was no fair.

See? A person could do multistep word problems even in an attitude tent. No biggie. You just had to have the right math-i-tude.

Not-So-Bad-i-tude

Judy Moody was down in the dumps. She had an attitude that was in the lower latitudes. A *bad-i-tude*.

"What's wrong?" Chloe asked her during tutoring that afternoon. "You hardly ate any of your pizza fractions."

"I have an attitude," said Judy.

"Everybody has an attitude," said Chloe. "It just means the way you think, the way you see things."

"The way I see things, Mrs Grossman doesn't like my attitude. Mrs Grossman says I need an attitude adjustment. So I went in the Attitude Tent, but all I got was a spider bite. All that did was adjust my attitude from bad to itchy."

"I know something that might help your attitude," said Chloe.

"Don't say algebra," said Judy.

"How would you like to come to college on Saturday?"

"Oh, no. You mean now I have to do maths at the weekend too?"

"Not for maths, silly. I mean, how would you like to come and spend the day with me at college? For fun."

Suddenly, she, Judy Moody, knew what an attitude adjustment felt like. It felt like when you went from a bad mood to a good mood. It felt like when your spider bite stopped itching. It felt like when you got to spend a whole, entire fun-not-maths day at college.

Judy could not wait for Saturday.

By mistake Judy woke up at six o'clock on Saturday morning, a not-school day. Chloe had told her that college kids like to sleep late, so Judy tried to think like a college kid and go back to sleep. But it was no use.

"I don't see what the big-whoop deal is about college," said Stink. "All they do is carry heavy books around and listen to headphones. And if you go to college, you have to sleep over without Mum and Dad for like three or four years. And you have to wash your own clothes!"

For a kid who read the encyclopedia, Stink sure didn't know a lot. "Stink, you don't have the right *attitude* for college. Just wait till you're older and wiser, like me."

"When I'm older and wiser, will I eat cereal with a fork too?"

"Oops," said Judy, opening the dishwasher to look for a spoon. By the time she got back to her bowl of cereal, her Mood Flakes had turned the milk pink.

Sweet! Pink milk (in Mood Flakes) was for *happy*. That was the first sign that she, Judy Moody, was about to have the time of her life.

Then Judy checked the Ask-a-Question Watch 5000 just to be sure.

Is today going to be the best day ever at college?

YUP!

She asked it again just to make sure and absolutely positive.

NO DOUBT!

It was a sign, all right. A sign to the power of three.

❂　　❂　　❂

Judy followed Chloe up to her third-floor dorm. The tiny room was chock-full of beds and desks and computers and books. Between bunk beds was an orange hairy rug, and on the beds were furry zebra-and-leopard-skin bedspreads. Posters covered the walls, even the ceiling.

There was a pink mini fridge and a mini TV and a mini microwave. Even a Bonjour Bunny alarm clock.

"Rare!" said Judy. "Your room is so orange and furry. Everything's cool-mini. You have a bunk bed like me, only yours has a desk under it. And you have the Bonjour Bunny alarm clock radio night light. Does it have a snooze button that lights up?"

A tall girl wearing pyjamas (same-same as Judy) came in and plopped down on a giant rubber-ball chair.

"Hey, roomie," Chloe said. "This is my

friend, Judy Moody. Judy, this is my room-mate Bethany Wigmore."

Bethany Wigmore had long, dark hair and large, dark eyes. Bethany Wigmore wore headphones and lots of necklaces. Bethany Wigmore had flip-flops with jewels on them!

"I like your flip-flops," Judy told her.

"Thanks. I made them."

"For serious?"

"It's easy," said Bethany Wigmore. "All you need are fake jewels and beads and a mini glue gun. C'mon, I'll show you."

Bethany Wigmore showed Judy Moody how to make fancified flip-flops. Then she said, "Now let's paint our toenails!"

"No, thanks," said Judy.

"We have *mood* nail polish," said Chloe. "It changes with your mood."

"I'm in!" said Judy. In no time, she, Judy Moody, had red-glitter toenails that turned purple. It was more impressive than rad, more powerful than rare. It was *sick-awesome. Mad-nasty!*

Who knew that having a roomie made life so way-not-boring?

"Let's food," said Chloe. "I'll take you to the dining room, Judy. Then you can come to class with me."

"Class?" Judy asked. *Class* sounded semi-boring, even though *college class* sounded like something she could brag about later.

"Painting class," said Chloe. "It'll be fun. I promise."

Bethany Wigmore called after them, "Hit me up later!"

❧ ❧ ❧

On the way to lunch, they passed a big green patch of grass in the middle of the campus called the Quad. Every inch of it was filled with tents. Judy had never seen so many attitude tents. Was everybody at college in a bad mood?

"Did all the kids in these tents get in to trouble and get sent to an attitude tent?" Judy asked.

"These aren't attitude tents," said Chloe. "This is a peace rally. Only instead of marching, people slept out in tents on the

Quad last night to make a statement saying that they're for peace."

"I guess you could say they rested in peace," said Judy, grinning.

"Good one," said Chloe. "C'mon, let's go and see my friend Paul."

There were drummers drumming and dancers dancing and people waving signs – all for peace. Chloe's friend Paul was one of the drummers. He let Judy make loads of noise on a bongo drum, and she got to hula hoop for peace and even tie-dye a T-shirt. On the front she drew a peace sign and wrote PEACE IS CRUCIAL.

They waited for Judy's T-shirt to dry, but Chloe finally said, "This is as much fun as

watching paint dry, huh? Let's check out the yoga tent."

The yoga tent had a very peace-full attitude. Judy learned to make shapes with her arms and legs. She got to pretend to be a cat, a mountain, a chair and a not-maths triangle.

"Who knew peace could be so much fun?" said Judy, wriggling her PEACE IS CRUCIAL T-shirt over her I ATE A SHARK T-shirt.

Next stop: cafeteria. Judy ate one pancake with three colours of syrup, a salad from the NOT-for-teachers-only salad bar and half of Chloe's burger, which was made of vegetables (minus aubergine). No lie!

She did not have to wait in line, she did not have to get bossed by bossy fifth-graders, and she did not have to eat boring old peanut butter and jam sandwiches that were so *babyish,* like at the cafe*terrible*. Who knew that veggies (smushed up on a bun with ketchup) could taste so *rad*?

Art-i-tude

"Oops, we'd better not be late for class," said Chloe. They raced across campus to the art block. Judy followed Chloe down a long corridor lined with colourful lockers. They passed a pottery class where people were spinning clay on wheels, a sculpture class where students were making buildings out of bubble wrap, and a … naked lady class!

Judy squeezed her eyes shut. "Please

tell me we are NOT going to Naked Lady Class."

Chloe almost spat out her coffee. "It's Life Drawing. To be an artist, you have to learn to draw real life."

"When I draw Real Life, it is NOT going to be bare-naked," said Judy.

In painting class, Judy got to sit next to Chloe in a dark room and watch a slide show of paintings. There were paintings of bones and giant sunflowers and swirly-twirly night skies. Even soup cans. There were paintings of paper leaves and moons, and paintings that looked like spilled cans of paint, even though the teacher (who everybody had to call professor) said it was a masterpiece. There were black-and-white paintings of birds that hurt your eyes if you stared at them too much.

"These paintings are psycho!" Judy said, cracking herself up. Chloe put her finger to her lips.

"In third grade, you're not allowed to talk when the teacher is talking either," Judy whispered. "Same-same!"

The teacher, Mr Professor-Who-Likes-Psycho-Paintings, was yacking on for ever about shadows in every picture. Shadows this and shadows that. Shadows here and shadows there. Shadows seemed to be very-way-important in art.

When the slide show and the yacking

were over, everybody got to make paintings of their own. (Finally!)

Judy got to stand next to Chloe at a
tall table and make a big giant mess. At
college, it did not matter if paper scraps
went all over the table. At college, it did
not matter if paint dripped all over the
floor. And at college, it did not matter how
many supplies you used, even a whole
entire bottle of sparkly-blue glitter glue.

Chloe said worrying about rules was
old skool. Chloe said art is life and life is
messy, so art should be messy.

At college, all that mattered was that
you: (1) use your imagination (which Judy
had loads and loads of) and (2) be yourself. Who else would she, Judy Moody, be?

Judy was so busy using her imagination and being herself that she made seven artworks in no time, including a monster Venus flytrap, a self-portrait cut into cubes and a bad-mood painting that looked a little like the spilled-can-of-paint-guy's masterpiece, with a dollop of Judy Moody thrown in.

Chloe was painting a bowl of cherries that were sitting on a stool.

"Are you still working on the same painting?" Judy asked.

"It takes a long time to paint a still life," said Chloe.

"Yeah, but you might want to try finishing it while you are *still* in this *life*.

It's only cherries." Judy turned her head sideways. "Or is it goldfish?"

"Thanks a lot," said Chloe.

"You should put some polka dots in the background," said Judy. "And it needs a cat or something."

Chloe said she liked Judy's ideas, but Judy did not see her painting any polka dots. Or cats. Just the same old cherries-not-goldfish bowl.

Judy picked up the squishy foam tray from underneath Chloe's real-life cherries. "Can I use this to make a pop-art painting like that Soup Can Guy?"

"Go for it," said Chloe.

A pop-art painting, Judy had just

learned, was a painting of an everyday object, something that you see all the time, like a can of soup, and don't even think about. Then when you paint it shocking pink or lemon yellow, all of a sudden it shocks you, and you think about it.

Judy pressed her pencil point into the foam tray to make the outline of a Band-Aid. Then she smeared the tray with paint and pressed it over and over nine times on to one big piece of paper in lots of different neon-bright colours.

"My pop art really pops!" Judy told Chloe.

"You did that?" said Chloe. "It looks fantastic! I mean it."

Chloe still had not painted one single polka dot. Not even a cat hair. "Haven't you finished yet?" Judy asked. "You are going to get an *S* for *Slow* or a *T* for *Turtle* in this class."

Chloe laughed. "OK, let's go. I can finish this later."

Judy gathered up all her paintings. "I'm going to hang them up in my bedroom, like an art show. I think this one's my best." She pointed at her pop-art painting. "I call it *Portrait of a Band-Aid-Not-Soup-Can without Shadows, Deluxe Edition.*"

"I like how you signed it just *Jude*," said Chloe.

"That's my artist name."

"Well, Just Jude, I think you'd better leave that one here, because it's not dry yet."

"Aw!" said Judy.

"Don't worry, I'll keep an eye on it for you. You can pick it up next time you come for tutoring. I'd better get you home. I have a twenty-page philosophy essay to write about Plato and Socrates."

Play-Doh and Soccer Teams? "Well, at least you get to write about *fun* stuff," said Judy.

"Yeah, right." As they climbed into Chloe's punch-buggy Gecko Green VW Beetle, she told Judy, "You busted that art class!"

"I owned it," Judy said, beaming from ear to ear.

As far as Judy could tell, there were only three bad things about college: (1) going to school on Saturday, (2) Naked Lady Class, and (3) yacking for a year and a day about shadows.

Other than that, college had hardly any rules, and you got to make a lot of noise about being peaceful. You got to have sleepovers every night with roomies like Bethany Wigmore and play drums with peeps like Paul and hang out in tents that did not have attitude and eat burgers made of veggies all day and change boring old ordinary stuff into art.

College was uber-*rare. Sick-awesome!*

Cat-i-tude

As soon as Judy got home from college, she asked Kate and Richard if she could have a pink mini fridge for her room. They said N-O. Judy called Chloe (for serious) on Kate's not-chocolate mobile phone.

"They actually think a *fridge* belongs in the *kitchen*," she told Chloe. *Old skool.*

The very next day, Judy took a long look around her room. It was *wearing sadface.* Time for a change. She would give her room a makeover – really *college* it up!

First, Judy piled tons of pillows on the floor. Next, she drew zebra stripes all over her duvet with a marker pen. Then Judy hung her paintings on the walls and even on the ceiling using Band-Aids for tape. She saved a place of honour over her bunk bed for *Portrait of a Band-Aid-Not-Soup-Can without Shadows, Deluxe Edition.*

Rad! All she needed now was a fuzzy, shaggy, hairy rug like Chloe's. But how to make a boring old un-fuzzy rug look like a beasty animal with jungle vibes?

She tried dust bunnies from under her bunk bed. She tried lint. She even tried getting Mouse to roll around on her rug to make it nice and cat-hairy.

Judy stood back to admire her new rug. It did not look like a tiger. It did not have jungle vibes. It looked like a giant hair ball. And to make matters worse, Kate made Judy vacuum it for *no* allowance.

Judy sat on her bottom bunk to think. Mouse was chasing a ball of wool. A ball of orange wool. A ball of fuzzy, hairy wool. "Mouse, give me that!" said Judy, chasing her around the room on hands and knees, knocking over piles of pillows and books and the rubbish bin.

"What's going on?" Stink asked. "What are you doing?"

"What's it look like I'm doing?" said Judy.

"Chasing the cat," said Stink. "But why are you chasing the cat?"

"To get the wool," said Judy.

"But why do you want the wool?" asked Stink.

"To cut it into a million little pieces."

"But why are you going to cut it into a million pieces?" Stink asked.

"To make a fuzzy orange rug. What do you think? I'm giving my room a hairy-rug makeover."

"*Mu-um!*" Stink yelled. "Judy's chasing the cat to get the wool to cut it into a million pieces to make a fuzzy rug to give her room a hairy-rug makeover!"

What an NCP.

After the hairy-rug makeover experiment, Judy went looking for a peaceful mood. "Peace out!" she called to anybody who was listening. "I'm going outside to the tent!"

The Toad Pee Club Tent was like the Attitude Tent without the attitude. Judy climbed inside, where it was secret and quiet, like the peace tents at college. She got down on her hands and knees. Mouse stood still on all fours, watching. Judy arched her back. Mouse arched her back. Judy breathed in and out. Mouse breathed in and out.

Judy gazed at her belly button. She tried to fill herself up with peace.

"What in the world...?" said Stink, barging into the tent.

"Stink, you're wrecking my peace."

"I'm wrecking your what?"

"It's yoga," said Judy. "Mouse and I are doing the cat pose."

"Mouse looks like a cat," said Stink, "but you just look like someone staring at her belly button upside down."

"Try it," Judy said. "I learned it at college."

"I can stare at my belly button sitting up," said Stink, "without going to college. Besides, staring at your belly button is about as much fun as watching paint dry."

"They do that at college too," said Judy.

"Bor-ing," said Stink.

"Hey, what's up?" asked Rocky and Frank, also barging into the tent with their big boy-feet.

"Oh, yeah," said Stink. "I came to tell you that Rocky and Frank are coming over."

"Is this an upside-down meeting of the Toad Pee Club?"

"It's yoghurt," said Stink. "She learned it at college."

"Yo-ga," said Judy. "Not yoghurt. It's like an exercise, not a snack food." Clearly Stink had never read the Y-for-*Yoga* encyclopedia.

"Show us," said Frank.

Judy showed them how to arch like a cat. She showed them how to bend in half like a chair, reach to the sky like a warrior and stand on one leg like a tree. "Now close your eyes, but don't think."

"I can't *not* think," said Frank. "I keep thinking how wacky it is to stand on one leg and pretend to be a tree and try not to think."

"I feel like a flamingo," said Stink. "Or a dorky stork."

"No talking," said Judy. She squeezed her eyes tighter.

CRASH! When Judy opened her eyes, the boys were a jumble of arms and legs on the ground, and they were laughing their heads off.

"Octopus pose!" said Stink, his legs sticking in the air.

"For your information, there's no such thing as an octopus pose."

Judy closed her eyes again and tried to hear quiet, but all she could hear was

more thrashing and crashing. She opened her eyes again.

Rocky had his neck stretched up to the ceiling. Frank had bendy knees and arms out like a monster. And Stink was all in a twisty ball.

"Giraffe pose," said Rocky.

"Superhero pose," said Frank.

"Human Pretzel pose," said Stink, cracking up.

"P.U.!" said Rocky, waving his hand in front of his face. "You should call that Passing Wind pose." The boys went wild.

"Oh, brother," said Judy. Boys were just plain no good at peace-full yoga.

Flunk-i-tude

When Judy got to Class 3T-now-3G the next morning, there was no teacher in the room. No teacher? No maths sweets on the desk? No Attitude Tent? Something was up. Way up!

The whole room was buzzing about what might have happened to Mrs Grossman. She went camping in her Attitude Tent? She ate too many good-behaviour sweets?

She ran away to Italy to be a better teacher?

Soon the bell rang. Still no teacher.

"Somebody has to be the teacher," said Jessica Finch, "and I think it should be me, since I'm brainiest."

"But Judy Moody's been to college!" yelled Frank.

"And she learned cool stuff," said Rocky, "like how to make yourself into a cat or a chair or a tree."

"Ju-dy Moo-dy! Ju-dy Moo-dy!" The class started yelling and stomping their feet.

She, Professor Judy Moody, stood in front of the whole class and told them all about college. She told about dorms and drums, veggie burgers and vending machines. She told about pancakes and pop art and peace tents. She led the whole class in a tree pose.

"And they learn Floss-O-Fee. It's not about cleaning your teeth. It's about thinking stuff till your head hurts, kind of like a brainteaser but more like a major head-scratcher."

"Like what?" asked Frank.

"Like … if a tree falls in the forest, OK, but nobody is around for miles and miles to hear it, does it still make a sound?"

The whole class went quiet. Peace-full quiet. Yoga-not-yoghurt quiet. The whole class was lost in a head-scratching attitude of thinking.

Just then, Judy caught a glimpse of

something in the corridor. Something like a shadow. The shadow moved. The shadow was...

"MR TODD!" Judy yelled, breaking the head-scratching silence. "Look, everybody! Professor Todd is back!"

"Mr Todd! Mr Todd!"

"Can I try your crutches?"

"Where's Mrs Grossman?"

"She gave us sweets."

"Except Judy, who had to sit in a tent all by herself."

When Class 3T-not-3G had settled down, Mr Todd told them about his broken foot and going to the doctor's and being late for school. He showed them his plaster cast, and all the kids got to sign it.

"I'm very proud of you, class, for the way you took over until I got here. And, Judy, you'll have to let me in on your secret," said Mr Todd. "I don't know how you got this class to be so quiet."

"It's college thinking!" said Frank. "Judy Moody goes to college AND third grade now."

They told Mr Todd everything about Mrs Grossman and the tutor and going to college. They told him about multistep word problems and maths sweets and the Attitude Tent.

Mr Todd smiled and frowned and raised his eyebrows and pushed up his glasses. "I sure missed a lot these last few weeks. Tell you what." He glanced at his watch.

"Looks like we've missed Spelling for today. So let's take a short break, and when we come back, it'll be time for maths. I'm going to pass out a quick quiz—"

"Not a test!"

"Don't worry. You won't be graded. I just want to see where everybody is in maths."

"Aww," everybody groaned. Everybody except Judy. She wanted to take the quiz. She wanted to show Mr Todd all the stuff she'd been learning with her tutor – graphs and fractions and algebra. For once, she'd be the one to win lots and lots and lots of maths sweets.

After break, Mr Todd passed out the tests. Judy got out her college-not-grouchy pencil for good luck. Third-grade pencils were *old skool*. Judy's college pencil flew. She only rubbed out twice. She even drew a graph for extra points. She did not look at her Ask-a-Question Watch 5000 once.

Judy busted that pop quiz. She owned that maths test. Mr Todd was going to be amazed at Judy's new math-i-tude. Soon she would be the proud owner of buckets of maths sweets.

Done! Judy looked up. She could not believe her eyes. She, Judy Maths-Genius Moody was not done first. She was *dead last*.

"Time's up!" said Mr Todd. "Let's have fifteen minutes of silent reading while I look over your papers."

For fifteen silent minutes, Judy read on in the *Catwings* book. She read with her eyes, but not with her brain. All her brain could think was how super-duper great she was going to be in maths.

Mr Todd was frowning. He looked up. He looked back down. Mr Todd scratched his head. Mr Todd frowned some more.

He wrote and wrote with his red pencil.

Judy could not help noticing he hardly even touched his green-for-good-work pencil.

"Class," said Mr Todd, looking up at last. "We have a problem."

Problem? Of course there was a problem. There were *ten* problems. Everybody knew maths was full of problems.

"I've corrected the papers, and the top score goes to Judy Moody."

"Woo-hoo!" said Judy. But she could not see how being top-of-her-class, best-ever in maths was a problem.

"The problem is ... everybody else failed."

What?! The whole, entire class flunked!

As in messed it up big time. As in got a big fat *F*.

"Most of you did not even finish your tests. And many of you did not even seem to try. Can anybody tell me what's going on here?"

The whole class looked down, staring at their desks, the floor, their shoes. Except for Judy.

"Professor Todd," said Judy, raising her hand. "I know what happened. I got to go to college and become an *uber*-genius in maths, and everybody else fell behind."

"Hmm," said Mr Todd. "Any other ideas? Jessica Finch?"

Jessica cleared her throat. "Well, um,

Rocky and Frank thought it would be way-cool to go to college, and they said—"

"It's our fault," said Rocky. "We thought if we all flunked, we would need a tutor and we would get to go to college too."

"Like Judy," said Frank.

"You mean you messed up on purpose?" Judy asked.

"Yeah, we just thought it up – during morning break," said Frank.

"Professor Todd!" said Judy. "I think I should get all the maths sweets, since I'm the only one who took the test for serious. And they should all go to the Attitude Tent."

"Let's get something straight," said Mr Todd. "I realize Mrs Grossman may have had different rules over the last few weeks. But in my class, we do our work to learn, not to earn sweets. As for the tent, well, it seems we have an attitude problem bigger than any tent."

Class 3T was silent. Not peace-full quiet. Itchy-scratchy quiet.

"We're sorry," said Frank.

"We'll take it again," said Rocky. "For real this time."

Mr Todd nodded.

"Professor Todd?" Judy asked. "I have a question. I mean, I was wondering – if you yelled at our class, but nobody was here to hear it, would it still mean you're angry with us?"

Grat-i-tude

"Mum! Dad!" Judy said at dinner that night. "I mean, Kate! Richard! Guess what! Professor Todd gave us a pop quiz in maths today, and I owned it. I only got one wrong, and I did the best of all my peeps and my whole entire class."

"Yeah, but everybody else flunked on purpose," said Stink, "because they all want to go to college too."

Eesh! Word sure travelled fast around Virginia Dare School.

"Who cares? It was *sooooo* money!" Judy said.

"She doesn't get money, does she?" asked Stink. "'Cos I'm good at maths, so if she gets money, I should get money too!"

"Stink, you're such a *geck*. And don't say, 'What's a geck?' Because that would make you more of a geck." Fact of Life: Stink = Geck. Geck = annoying person!

"Nobody's getting any money," said Dad.

"And nobody's a geck," said Mum.

"Yeah, you're not at college now," Stink said.

"Good news, though," said Mum. "You won't have to have a tutor any more."

"Yeah, no more yoghurt!" said Stink.

"Huh?" Judy loved college. She liked having a tutor.

"You knew this was just for a short time," Dad said. "To get extra help for a few weeks. But now Mr Todd's back, and we're proud of how well you're doing."

"You'll still see Chloe, honey," Mum said. "Maybe she'll come to your class to help Mr Todd. And she said she'd be happy to babysit any time."

"Does she know Stink lives here too?"

"And that's not even the best news," said Mum. "When Chloe called today—"

"Chloe called? You talked to Chloe? When? Where was I?"

"You were at school—" said Mum.

"No fair." Judy couldn't help it if her mobile phone was made of chocolate.

"Let Mum finish," said Dad.

"Anyway, remember a painting you made when you went to college for a day with Chloe?"

"Yes! *Portrait of a Band-Aid-Not-Soup-Can without Shadows, Deluxe Edition.*"

"What's that?" Stink asked.

"It's a pop-art painting like that guy who paints cans of soup, Andy Warthog."

Stink snorted like a warthog.

"Warhol," said Dad. "Andy Warhol."

"Is anybody going to let me finish?" Mum asked.

"Peace!" said Judy, holding up two fingers.

"As I was saying, I guess you left it there to dry, and the professor thought the painting had been done by one of his college students. He chose your painting to hang in an art show at the college. They have a small gallery in the library there."

She, Judy Moody, could not believe her ears. "Painting? College? Art show? Me?" she asked.

Dad laughed. "We thought you'd be pleased."

Pleased? Pleased was a teeny-tiny fraction of what she felt. This was *uber*-exciting.

This was ridonkulus-rare. She, Judy Moody Warthog, aka Just Jude, was going to be in an art show *at college*! For serious!

"I have to call Chloe," Judy said.

"On your chocolate mobile phone?" Stink asked.

"Stink. I take it back. You're not just a geck. You're a geck squared. Geck to the power of three."

"Gecko-gecko, click-click, cheep-cheep-cheep," sang Stink, bobbing his head and making gecko noises all around the living room.

What a warthog.

❧   ❧   ❧

The next morning at school, Judy flip-flopped down the corridor to Room 3T.

"Professor Todd?" Judy asked. "Did you tell Kate and Richard that I don't need a tutor any more? Because I really learned a lot at college and I'd like to keep going. And besides, my painting is in an art show there, and I'd really like to see—"

"You know, Judy, you're not the only one who wants to go to college," said Mr Todd.

"What do you mean? Didn't you already go to college, like a long time ago, I mean, to be a teacher and everything?"

"Not me – the class. Class 3T is going to college."

"You mean the whole class needs a

tutor? But I thought everybody just flunked the test on purpose."

"Not for tutoring," said Mr Todd. "We're going on a school trip."

"To college?"

"To college," said Mr Todd.

"And Chloe will be there?"

"Chloe will be there. We'll be spending a whole morning in the Maths Department."

"And we can go and see my painting?"

"We can go and see your painting. Won't that be exciting?"

"You don't know the half of it! The three-quarters of it. The nine-tenths of it. Thank you, Mr Todd, thank you!"

She, Judy Moody, had a brand-new attitude. It was *grat*-i-tude.

Glad-i-Tude

One whole week had to go by before Judy Moody got to go to college with her class. The week took about a year. At last it was time.

When Class 3T got to college, their first stop was the Maths Department. Judy took everyone over to the Investigation Station and showed them how to build with sponge blocks and draw graphs and play Tic-Tac-Cookie. They even got a taste of

Chloe's special pizza fractions (minus the pizza tables, which Judy got to collect).

Then Chloe passed out poster boards. Everyone got to spread out all over the floor and make their very own board games. Judy Moody drew lots of different tents on her board and a twisty-turny path that connected them.

Chloe peeked over her shoulder. "What are these?" she asked.

"See, you start out in the Attitude Tent," said Judy. "The object of the game is to try not to land in the Bad-i-tude Tent. To win, you have to get all the way to the Glad-i-tude Tent."

Next, she made a spinner. Then she made up Attitude Cards.

"See, bad stuff can happen to you along the way," said Judy. "But it all depends on your attitude. If you pick a bad Attitude Card, you have to go to the Bad-i-tude Tent. If you pick a good Attitude Card, you get to skip way ahead. Three good Attitude Cards, and you win the Peace Prize."

"Rad!" said Chloe.

"See," said Judy, "in the Judy Moody game of life, it's all about attitude."

❧   ❧   ❧

"Time for lunch!" Chloe called. Chloe and Mr Todd carried big boxes over to the picnic tables by the duck pond. Class 3T counted twelve shiny green-headed ducks, twenty-seven Canadian geese, three regular duck bottoms and eleven turtles.

"We could draw a graph!" said Judy.

"Let's eat first," said Mr Todd. Chloe passed round lunch boxes. Inside each box was ... a veggie burger. Soon, Class 3T was yoga-quiet as they vegged out on veggie burgers and smoothies. And the ducks vegged out on all the breadcrumbs they dropped.

"Yum! Bet you didn't know that healthy food actually tasted good," said Judy.

"And for dessert," said Chloe, "everybody gets a cone of Screamin' Mimi's Rain Forest Mist ice cream."

"Blue ice cream!"

"YAY!"

"It's my favourite!"

"Is it made of vegetables too?"

When everybody had finished licking the last drops of ice cream, Frank asked Chloe, "Do you have break at college?"

"Sure," said Chloe. "At college, you can make your own breaks, any time you want. Just about."

"Whoa," said Judy and Rocky and Frank.

Across the field, Judy saw two college kids walking towards them. They were carrying Frisbees and hula hoops and ... drums!

"Hey," said Judy, pointing, "it's Bethany Wigmore and Paul the drummer guy."

Class 3T had the best break ever – break squared, college style. When they had finished hula-hooping and drumming and chasing after Frisbees, it was time to go and see the art show.

Judy Moody and Class 3T walked across the Quad, round Coffee Catz and past the art block to the library. Quietly, they filed up the stairs to the second-floor art gallery.

Mum was there, and Dad, and Stink with a camera!

"What are you guys doing here?" Judy whispered.

"We didn't want to miss your big show," said Dad.

"And I got out of learning about commas!" said Stink.

Judy stepped inside the quiet room, where paintings lined the white walls.

There were still lifes of fruit and landscapes of trees. There were paintings of blobs and cut-out paper collages of cats.

Then she saw it. *Portrait of a Band-Aid-Not-Soup-Can without Shadows, Deluxe Edition.*

"Guess which one's mine," said Judy.

"The Band-Aids!" Stink shouted, running up to the painting.

"It certainly is colourful," said Dad.

"Creative," said Mum.

"Very college," said Mr Todd, winking.

"Look!" said Stink. "You got a ribbon."

"Me? Best in Show?" Judy asked.

Stink peered closer at the ribbon. "Never mind," he said, blocking it with his big head so Judy couldn't see.

"What?" Judy asked. "Let me see."

"You don't want to see," said Stink. "It says you got HORRIBLE MENTION. That really stinks."

"Horrible Mention?" She, Judy Moody, won the prize for the most horrible painting in the art show? "Why even *mention* it if it's *horrible*?" she wailed.

Mr Todd laughed. So did Mum and Dad. So did Chloe.

"Why is everybody laughing?" Judy asked. "Horrible Mention means they think my painting is horrible."

"It's an *Honourable* Mention," Chloe explained.

Honourable Mention sounded way better than Horrible Mention. "That's good, right?" Judy said. Stink moved over so Judy could see.

"Wicked good," said Chloe. "It means your painting was so rad, they thought they should *honour* it with a big fat ribbon."

Sick-awesome!

"Let's stand next to your painting so we can take a picture," said Mum. Everybody crowded around Judy, and the library lady snapped a picture on Stink's camera.

"Let me see!" said Judy.

She peered at the image on the camera. Next to her and all around her were Kate and Richard and Stink; Rocky, Frank, Jessica Finch and the rest of Class 3T; Professor Todd and Chloe; even Paul the Drummer.

In the very centre, right in front of her Not-Horrible-Mention painting, stood Judy herself, smiling from ear to ear.

If that picture were a painting, she, Judy Moody, would give it a name. *Portrait of the Artist with the 'Rents, the Professor, the College Tutor, a Few Peeps and the Geck, with Shadows, Deluxe Edition.*

It was only a split-second, one-sixtieth-of-a-minute, a giga-flip-flop moment in Judy Moody's own personal game of life, but it felt big. She, Judy Moody, was filled with *glad*-i-tude.

Rad-i-tude!

Judy Moody's Not-Webster's FIRST

the bomb = the best

busted = did well; *owned*

RAD!

crucial = *Rare!* Excellent! Awesome!

for serious = for real

geck = annoying person = Stink

OLD SKOOL

hit me up later = call me later; see you later

let's food = let's eat

mad-nasty = see *sick-awesome*

GECK!

natch = of course; naturally

NCP = nincompoop; a silly or foolish person

old skool = old-fashioned; out of date

owned = ruled

paper (verb) = write a report

Natch!

CRUCIAL

New World College Dictionary
EDITION

peace out = goodbye; I'm leaving

peeps = friends

rad = radical; *crucial*

'rents; 'rentals = parents

ridonkulus = ridiculous

roomie = roommate

sick-awesome = more impressive than *rad*;

more powerful than *rare*

so money = excellent

uber = way-cool; over-the-top awesome

wearing sadface = sadly lacking;

looking unhappy

wicked good = better than good

'RENTS

PEEPS

Roomie

SoMoney

UBER!

PEACE OUT!